# That Pretty Pretty; or, The Rape Play

by
Sheila Callaghan

A Samuel French Acting Edition

SAMUELFRENCH.COM

Copyright © 2009 by Sheila Callaghan

*ALL RIGHTS RESERVED*

Cover photo by Sandra Coudert
Actors pictured: Lisa Joyce, Danielle Slavick, Joseph Gomez and Greg Keller

CAUTION: Professionals and amateurs are hereby warned that *THAT PRETTY PRETTY; OR, THE RAPE PLAY* is subject to a Licensing Fee. It is fully protected under the copyright laws of the United States of America, the British Commonwealth, including Canada, and all other countries of the Copyright Union. All rights, including professional, amateur, motion picture, recitation, lecturing, public reading, radio broadcasting, television and the rights of translation into foreign languages are strictly reserved. In its present form the play is dedicated to the reading public only.

The amateur live stage performance rights to *THAT PRETTY PRETTY; OR, THE RAPE PLAY* are controlled exclusively by Samuel French, Inc., and licensing arrangements and performance licenses must be secured well in advance of presentation. PLEASE NOTE that amateur Licensing Fees are set upon application in accordance with your producing circumstances. When applying for a licensing quotation and a performance license please give us the number of performances intended, dates of production, your seating capacity and admission fee. Licensing Fees are payable one week before the opening performance of the play to Samuel French, Inc., at 45 W. 25th Street, New York, NY 10010.

Licensing Fee of the required amount must be paid whether the play is presented for charity or gain and whether or not admission is charged.

Stock licensing fees quoted upon application to: Samuel French, Inc. 45 W. 25th Street, New York, NY 10010. For all other rights than those stipulated above, apply to: The Gersh Agency, 41 Madison Avenue, New York, NY 10010 Att: Seth Glewen.

Particular emphasis is laid on the question of amateur or professional readings, permission and terms for which must be secured in writing from Samuel French, Inc.

Copying from this book in whole or in part is strictly forbidden by law, and the right of performance is not transferable.

Whenever the play is produced the following notice must appear on all programs, printing and advertising for the play: "Produced by special arrangement with Samuel French, Inc."

Due authorship credit must be given on all programs, printing and advertising for the play.

**ISBN 978-0-573-69690-9**

No one shall commit or authorize any act or omission by which the copyright of, or the right to copyright, this play may be impaired.

No one shall make any changes in this play for the purpose of production.

Publication of this play does not imply availability for performance. Both amateurs and professionals considering a production are strongly advised in their own interests to apply to Samuel French, Inc., for written permission before starting rehearsals, advertising, or booking a theatre.

No part of this book may be reproduced, stored in a retrieval system, or transmitted in any form, by any means, now known or yet to be invented, including mechanical, electronic, photocopying, recording, videotaping, or otherwise, without the prior written permission of the publisher.

## MUSIC USE NOTE

Licensees are solely responsible for obtaining formal written permission from copyright owners to use copyrighted music in the performance of this play and are strongly cautioned to do so. If no such permission is obtained by the licensee, then the licensee must use only original music that the licensee owns and controls. Licensees are solely responsible and liable for all music clearances and shall indemnify the copyright owners of the play and their licensing agent, Samuel French, Inc., against any costs, expenses, losses and liabilities arising from the use of music by licensees.

## IMPORTANT BILLING AND CREDIT REQUIREMENTS

All producers of *THAT PRETTY PRETTY; OR, THE RAPE PLAY must* give credit to the Author of the Play in all programs distributed in connection with performances of the Play, and in all instances in which the title of the Play appears for the purposes of advertising, publicizing or otherwise exploiting the Play and/or a production. The name of the Author *must* appear on a separate line on which no other name appears, immediately following the title and *must* appear in size of type not less than fifty percent of the size of the title type.

In addition the following credit *must* be given in all programs and publicity information distributed in association with this piece:

World premiere produced by Rattlestick Playwrights Theater.
*That Pretty Pretty, or The Rape Play* was developed with support From Playwrights Foundation, San Francisco, CA and Salvage Vanguard, Austin, TX

***THAT PRETTY PRETTY; OR, THE RAPE PLAY*** has been workshopped at the William Inge Center for the Arts (Peter Ellenstein, artistic director) in Independence, Kansas (2007), the "In the Rough" series at Playwrights Foundation (Amy Mueller, artistic director; Jonathan Spector, associate artistic director) in San Francisco, CA (2008) and at the Salvage Vanguard Theatre (Brad Carlin, executive director; Jenny Larson, artistic director) in Austin, TX (2008).

The world premiere of ***THAT PRETTY PRETTY; OR, THE RAPE PLAY*** was produced by Rattlestick Playwrights Theater in New York City (David Van Asselt, artistic director; Sandra Coudert, managing director) and opened on February 10, 2009. The production was directed by Kip Fagan; set design was by Narelle Sissons, costume design was by Jessica Pabst, lighting design was by Matt Frey, sound design was by Eric Shim, hair and makeup design was by Erin Kennedy Lunsford; the production stage manager was Katrina Renee Herrmann. The cast was as follows:

**RODNEY** . . . . . . . . . . . . . . . . . . . . . . . . . . . . . . . . . . . . . . . . . . . Joseph Gomez
**AGNES** . . . . . . . . . . . . . . . . . . . . . . . . . . . . . . . . . . . . . . . . . . . . . Lisa Joyce
**OWEN** . . . . . . . . . . . . . . . . . . . . . . . . . . . . . . . . . . . . . . . . . . . . Greg Keller
**JANE FONDA** . . . . . . . . . . . . . . . . . . . . . . . . . . . . . . . . . . . . Annie McNamara
**VALERIE** . . . . . . . . . . . . . . . . . . . . . . . . . . . . . . . . . . . . . . . . . Danielle Slavick

**NOTE:** The section of the play where the women throw themselves onto the ground in choreographed fits is an edited excerpt from Charles L. Mee's play *Big Love*.

## CHARACTERS

**AGNES**
**VALERIE**
**RODNEY**
**OWEN**
**JANE FONDA / JANE**

### AUTHOR'S NOTE

A stroke (/) marks the point of interruption in overlapping dialogue. When the stroke is not immediately followed by text, the next line should occur on the last syllable of the word before the slash – not an overlap but a concise interruption

### With Special Thanks to...

Chad Beckim, Molly Pearson, Erica Gould, Sharon Freedman, Cynthia Silver, Di Johnston, Vincent Madero, Greg Keller, Alexander Alioto, Sarah Malkin, Jessa Sherman, Paola Grande, Gregory Moss, S. Parker Leventer, Howard Stern, Raymi the Minx, Mark Christian Subias, Travis York, David Brooks, Lula Graves, Alissa Ford, Jennifer Morris, Paul Willis, Daniel Manley, Adrien-Alice Hansel, Rebecca Hart, Joseph Gomez, Cory Hinkle, Rory Lipede, Amanda White, Deb Fink, Juliet Tanner, Davina Cohen, Anil Margsahayam, Anthony Nemirovsky, Sandra Coudert, David Van Asselt, Kip Fagan, Lisa Joyce, Danielle Slavick, Annie McNamara, Joe Gomez, Peter Eleenstein, William Inge Center for the Arts, New Dramatists, and Daniel Talbot.

## PROLOGUE

*(VALERIE and AGNES appear in the darkness, face-forward. Single lights come up on each. Something like Bon Jovi's "You Give Love a Bad Name" plays faintly in the background. A fellow croons along dismally and drunkenly with the song.\*)*

**AGNES.** Val?

**VALERIE.** Yeah?

**AGNES.** I'm a little drunk.

**VALERIE.** You drink too much.

**AGNES.** What state are we in?

**VALERIE.** You're a dumbass.

**AGNES.** We've done this a lot.

**VALERIE.** I know.

**AGNES.** We're gonna run out of states.

**VALERIE.** Dumbass Supreme. We still have Colorado, Delaware, Michigan, Louisiana, Alabama, Arkansas, / Cincinnati, Missouri, Nebraska, North Carolina…

**AGNES.** Then we'll get caught. Or something. I don't want…um…

**VALERIE.** I thought we didn't care if we got caught.

**AGNES.** We just…wanna keep going for as long as we can. Because we fucking HATE THEM ALL. Okay. Not just the ones with bombs in their trunks.

**VALERIE.** That's right.

**AGNES.** And we hate fucking people telling us how to act.

**VALERIE.** Right.

**AGNES.** About our bodies.

**VALERIE.** Right.

**AGNES.** And the internet.

\*See Music Use Note on page 3.

**VALERIE.** Sure.

**AGNES.** And the radio. I'm hungry.

**VALERIE.** You're always hungry.

**AGNES.** The food sucks here. And there's none left.

**VALERIE.** You have a problem.

**AGNES.** If there was more food I wouldn't be drunk because I would of eaten enough and the food would be absorbing the vodka. When you wanna go over?

**VALERIE.** When he finishes his karaoke song.

**AGNES.** Right on. *(beat, tone change)* Sometimes I think you love me too much.

*(a long beat)*

**VALERIE.** Delete delete delete delete delete delete delete.

## End of Prologue

*(lights up)*

*(**VALERIE** and **AGNES** stumble into a posh hotel room in fur coats. **AGNES** is wearing a bonnet and **VALERIE** a straw hat. Beneath their coats their outfits are outrageously skimpy.)*

*(Something feels very fake about the whole setup…perhaps the set is too vivid, perhaps everyone is a little too enthusiastic.)*

*(The acting in the following scene should be completely and artificially over-the-top intense. Lots of volume.)*

**AGNES.** Where is he you fucking lost him / already.

**VALERIE.** He was right behind you don't freak on me.

**AGNES.** He's mine Val.

**VALERIE.** Where's the minibar…ROCK!

*(**VALERIE** goes to the minifridge.)*

**AGNES.** HE'S MINE / VALERIE

**VALERIE.** Shhhh.

*(**AGNES** tosses herself on the bed and begins bouncing. **VALERIE** cannot open the minifridge.)*

**AGNES.** I'm the 'ho here. Just remember that. This bed smells like starch and marinated ass…I like hotels I like hotels I like hotels.

**VALERIE.** Locked? Fuck…

*(**RODNEY** stumbles in behind them. He is red-faced and wears a tie and a sombrero.)*

**RODNEY.** Wasted!

**AGNES.** Wasted!

*(**RODNEY** falls on the bed on top of **AGNES**.)*

**RODNEY.** This place is decent…

**AGNES.** My uncle works for the chain.

*(They begin to kiss.)*

**VALERIE.** Hey. HEY. Hey Agnes. Show him your new dance, you slutty whore.

**AGNES.** I made up a dance.

**RODNEY.** Go on.

**VALERIE.** Slutty little whore.

**AGNES.** I don't have a name yet for it.

**RODNEY.** Do they have whiskey?

**VALERIE.** I can't get the fucker open...

(**VALERIE** *kicks the minibar furiously. It swings open. She begins rooting around inside.*)

**AGNES.** You aren't watching...

**VALERIE.** Go.

(**AGNES** *does a complicated hip-hop move.* **RODNEY** *applauds.*)

**VALERIE.** She made it for Howard Stern.

**AGNES.** Shut UP.

**VALERIE.** She thinks if she can get on the air, he'll ask her to dance.

**AGNES.** Most people think he's gross but he's got these ice blue eyes, that's why he wears sunglasses all the time.

(**VALERIE** *pulls out a digital camera and begins shooting pictures of the room.*)

**AGNES.** You're like psycho with that shit.

**VALERIE.** For the blog...

(**VALERIE** *aims the camera at* **AGNES**. **AGNES** *giggles and begins to strip.*)

**RODNEY.** You girls aren't really sisters, are you...

**AGNES.** We came out of the same womb...

**RODNEY.** You're wild. You are wild.

**VALERIE.** Are you two ready to kick it or will I stand here like a douche bag?

(**AGNES** *begins to take off her bonnet.*)

**RODNEY.** Leave the bonnet on.

(**AGNES** *and* **RODNEY** *begin to maul each other.* **VALERIE** *lights a cigarette and watches.*)

**AGNES.** She's letting me have you first, she NEVER does that.

**RODNEY.** *(to* **VALERIE***)* Come here…

**VALERIE.** I'm fine.

**RODNEY.** I paid for both…

**AGNES.** Come on Val…

**VALERIE.** I'm thirsty…I'm going outside for a / Diet Coke.

**RODNEY.** Do not leave the fucking room.

*(Beat.* **VALERIE** *reaches into her purse and pulls out a gun.)*

**RODNEY.** Wait.

*(***VALERIE** *shoots* **RODNEY** *in the head. Blood hits the wall and the floor.)*

**AGNES.** GROSS. Gross gross gross get him off me…

*(***VALERIE** *helps get* **RODNEY** *off* **AGNES**. *They roll him onto the floor.)*

**AGNES.** You're kind of harsh sometimes. Get one for the blog.

*(***VALERIE** *shoots a picture of the dead* **RODNEY**.*)*

**AGNES.** Should I get in it, too?

**VALERIE.** Yeah…pose a little.

*(***AGNES** *starts to remove the bonnet.)*

**VALERIE.** Keep the fucking bonnet on.

*(***VALERIE** *begins snapping photos of* **AGNES** *in various poses with the dead* **RODNEY**.*)*

**AGNES.** I hate fat people. There were SO MANY fat people tonight. The women all wore dainty little boots with little toothpick heels and they had fucking ENORMOUS cankles…And the FUCKING HATS!! What's the point of a hat party, even?

**VALERIE.** It wasn't a hat party, dumbass. It was a benefit.

**AGNES.** I've been to benefits where they didn't bring out a barrel of hats. Who the fuck gave those right-wing fucks the idea they'd have more fun with hats on their fat fucking heads? Hey. Jesus had a beard, right?

**VALERIE.** Yeah.

**AGNES.** I pictured him clean-shaven for a second. I wish we had gotten there before all the food got eaten…I want new breasts, do you think we can buy me some?

**VALERIE.** You don't need them anymore.

**AGNES.** I may have quit stripping but I still like my body to look slammin'…

**VALERIE.** Make him talk.

(**AGNES** *grabs hold of* **RODNEY**'s *bottom lip.*)

**AGNES.** "Fetus fetus fetus fetus holy fucking shit I love the fetus and Jesus loves the fetus too, and just remember it ain't where life begins but where LOVE begins…" You could have let me fuck him first, Val. I was getting wet and everything…

**VALERIE.** He's a lousy lay…

**AGNES.** You can't tell by just looking at him.

**VALERIE.** He's got a cashew dick. Look.

(**AGNES** *checks it out.*)

**AGNES.** How did you know?

**VALERIE.** I did him in the bathroom while you were on the buffet table.

**AGNES.** You wouldn't.

**VALERIE.** Who asked you to get up on the goddamn buffet table, Agnes? Who asked you to do that?

**AGNES.** I had something to say.

**VALERIE.** You make an ass of yourself when you stand on a buffet table. You make like you have no self-respect. That is tedious and it's UGLY.

**AGNES.** Just because I don't have a blog doesn't mean I don't have something to say.

**VALERIE.** And no one heard you over the Quiet Riot. And you could have slipped and fallen, like that time on your garage door.

(*They stare at each other a moment. Something subtle changes in* **VALERIE**.)

*(She opens her computer and begins to type furiously.* **AGNES** *does not hear her speak.)*

**VALERIE.** Words words words. Come on, sucka. This gal is a real beeyotch. BITCH SUPREME. Talkin' shit about her manifesto…ridding the world of shitbags trying to jam their laws into her uterus. Lots of fucks. Fuck fuck fuck. What else…OH! She's a secret dyke! HA, YES!!! Wants to get her freak on with Agnes! But wait, they're sisters. Think on this, come back to it later. Maybe she should be more angry, or like. Oh, and super hot. A super hot angry dyke. She's a HATER. RAAAR! YEAH!! LIKE AN ANIMAL!!!

*(***VALERIE*** *springs up from her chair.)*

**AGNES.** Where are you going?

**VALERIE.** DIET COKE!

**AGNES.** From where?

**VALERIE.** VENDING MACHINE!

**AGNES.** Get me a seltzer please.

**VALERIE.** IF THEY DON'T HAVE?

**AGNES.** Diet Coke.

*(***VALERIE*** *leaves.* **AGNES** *manipulates* **RODNEY**'s *mouth again.)*

**AGNES.** "She smelled like grilled cheese and mustard." Man I'm hungry. Wonder if they do room service here. But wait! I don't eat. I am a crazy skinny obsessed monster. AND, I spend my days and nights plotting on how to be a skinnier version of myself…Also, I have a lot of sex with men who aren't my boyfriend. Sometimes my boyfriend loves me too much, and that makes me go ape-shit with other guys. Maybe I'm afraid of commitment. Maybe that's why I hate on these dudes. At any rate, I have no self-respect. Awesome.

*(***AGNES*** *straddles* **RODNEY**'s *leg and begins humping it.)*

*(***VALERIE*** *returns with two Diet Cokes.)*

**AGNES.** Val...do the other leg...

**VALERIE.** Uh-uh.

**AGNES.** Come on...

**VALERIE.** I'm drinking my Diet Coke.

>   (**VALERIE** *connects her camera to the computer.* **AGNES** *grabs* **RODNEY**'s *bottom lip again as she humps.*)

**AGNES.** "I like really skinny girls. How'd you get so fucking skinny..."
Starving myself and drinking water and longboarding my face off...I can't wait till summer...my metabolism speeds up in the summer...I'd burn more calories during sex if it took me longer to get off...

**VALERIE.** Then take longer...

**AGNES.** I...can't...

>   (**AGNES** *climaxes.* **VALERIE** *hands* **AGNES** *a Diet Coke.*)

**VALERIE.** The ice machine was broken. Hundred-fifty a room, you'd think you could...wait a second. *(tone change)* RAR! HUNDRED-FIFTY A ROOM, YOU'D THINK YOU COULD GET SOME FUCKING ICE!

**AGNES.** Complain to the management.

>   (**VALERIE** *picks up the phone and dials zero.*)

**VALERIE.** HI...YEAH, THE ICE MACHINE ISN'T WORKING, COCKWEED! ...NO, JUST HALF A BUCKET IS FINE...THANKS, COCKWEED.

*(She hangs up.)*

**VALERIE.** HE'LL BE RIGHT UP!

**AGNES.** You didn't call / him

**VALERIE.** *(tegarding her computer)* ROCKNESS!! THEY HAVE WIFI! *(typing)* Rockness, bitches...I'm the Rockness Monster...

>   (**AGNES** *is bored.*)

**AGNES.** I should piss the bed. Dare me?

>   (**AGNES** *jumps on the bed and drops her pants.*)

**AGNES.** Dare me, quick! 'Cause even if you don't I'll still do it…

**VALERIE.** I dare you.

*(AGNES tries to pee.)*

**AGNES.** Pee, pee…Ssssss…argh, performance anxiety!!! Wait…there's a trickle…

*(AGNES pees on the bed.)*

**AGNES.** I'M PEEING IN THE BED! I'M PEEING IN THE BED! HOW FUCKING AWESOME IS THAT?

**VALERIE.** Completely.

*(Beat. AGNES is bored again.)*

**AGNES.** You think there's a piano here?

**VALERIE.** No.

**AGNES.** I love to play the piano. I dream of dinner parties and fancy linens, I dream of myself playing piano beautifully afterwards, like a recital, with everyone applauding. So classy.

*(beat)*

**AGNES.** *(simultaneously)* Shit. I'm not at all classy. I'm a skanky 'ho. I secretly think it would make me like, elegant if I could play like, really really well. That's deep. And messed up. How the fuck am I gonna pull that off? More on this later.

**VALERIE.** *(simultaneously)* Shit. You're not at all classy. You're a skanky 'ho. You secretly think it would make you like, elegant if you could play like, really really well. How the fuck am I gonna pull that off?

*(In the following, underlined words are spoken by both women.)*

**AGNES.** Do they get Howard Stern in Mississippi?

**VALERIE.** I AM SO FUCKING SICK OF HEARING ABOUT HOWARD FUCKING STERN!! Too angry? Too angry?

**AGNES.** Oh damn. He's on Sirius. I need Satellite to get him. Do I have Satellite?

**VALERIE.** You are dumber than a bag of dumb, Agnes. You should have the word DUMBASS tattooed across your forehead so when dudes fuck you they won't think they're fucking the smart out of you. *(tone change)* That's really harsh. Agnes isn't retarded, or. She's just like, manipulative. I'm losing it.

**AGNES.** I'm not retarded. I'm just manipulative. My dumbness is like, a cover. I'm conflicted, therefore I hide behind stupidity. Ooh, folksy. Work that. Hey Valerie. When you were fucking my husband, did he talk about God at all?

**VALERIE.** Which time?

**AGNES.** The last time.

*(VALERIE says nothing. AGNES grabs her own bottom lip.)*

**AGNES.** "No Agnes. He was talking about you."

**VALERIE.** No Agnes. He was talking about you.

**AGNES.** Okay.

**VALERIE.** Okay. Wait. No. Who was fucking who's / husband?

**AGNES.** Who was fucking who's husband?

**VALERIE.** I'm losing it. I gotta change it up. Okay, let's get SUBTEXTY. The STAKES HAVE BEEN RAISED!

*(AGNES and VALERIE become a bad Pinter play.)*

**AGNES.** What did you think of the DJ?

*(beat)*

**VALERIE.** He was all right.

*(beat)*

**AGNES.** I love 80s rock.

*(beat)*

**VALERIE.** Do you?

*(As an answer, AGNES jumps up on top of the bed and begins singing "Still of the Night" by Whitesnake, and miming David Coverdale from the video.\* This is an act of aggression, but it is super sexy. She mimes a guitar. VALERIE watches her.)*

---

\*See Music Use Note on page 3.

**AGNES.** Remember in the video, the guitar solo, it gets all smoky he's like shadowy and silhouettey and on his knees, and he whips out a fucking BOW, like for a violin, and starts BOWING his guitar on his knees and practically humping the guitar…I would get off to that like twice an hour.

**VALERIE.** You are so pretty. *(beat)* FUCK! Damnit, Agnes! You see what you do? "Wah, you're so pretty, wah…" Like a cancer. Bulldog, where's the bulldog? KEEP THE FUCKING BULLDOG!

*(**VALERIE** barks like a rabid dog.)*

**AGNES.** Is it working?

**VALERIE.** I don't know.

**AGNES.** Can I do something?

**VALERIE.** Hit me in the face. Get me angry, get me all riled up.

**AGNES.** Fist or palm?

**VALERIE.** Fist. No, palm.

*(**AGNES** hits **VALERIE** in the face.)*

**VALERIE.** Again.

*(**AGNES** hits **VALERIE** in the face.)*

**VALERIE.** Try to get your ring into it.

*(**AGNES** turns her ring around on her finger and hits **VALERIE** again.)*

**VALERIE.** Am I bleeding?

**AGNES.** No.

**VALERIE.** One more.

*(**AGNES** hits **VALERIE** in the face.)*

**VALERIE.** Okay.

**AGNES.** You mad?

**VALERIE.** Yeah.

**AGNES.** Furious?

**VALERIE.** Yeah, yeah. Thanks.

(AGNES *hits* VALERIE *in the face again.*)

VALERIE. Enough!

AGNES. Hit me back!

VALERIE. Later…I need to ride this out…

(AGNES *sulks on the bed.* VALERIE *is about to type.*)

VALERIE. Kick it, homes…smack that juicy groove…

(*She types nothing. Beat.*)

VALERIE. (*forlorn*) I'm lost.

(*An über-chipper* JANE FONDA *enters, dressed in leg warmers and a headband. She begins doing aerobics for us.*)

VALERIE. Jane Fonda…thank God.

JANE FONDA. My workout is designed to build strength, develop flexibility and increase endurance. To get the full benefit from the workout you must do it with me from beginning to end without stopping. It is this vigorous and sustained use of your entire body that will not only tone your muscles but will burn up calories, improve your circulation, eliminate toxins and strengthen your heart and lungs. The basis of the workout is the repetition of certain movements that use a single muscle group against the resistance of your own body weight. (*demonstrating*) You see how excellent I am? An inspiration. Generations of women look up to me. Do I inspire fear in you? I shouldn't. Glow glow glow, sparkle like a star. I am not someone who dominates. I am frank and dignified. I am sincere. I have loads of confidence, except when I feel abused, and then I simply raise my chin and take it. THAT'S a real woman. THAT'S heroic. And I have a kickin' bod.

(JANE FONDA *continues an aerobics routine to "Pretty Baby" by Kay Starr. She does an aerobics-ey soft shoe.* VALERIE *and* AGNES *join her soft shoe dance, then they all sing "Pretty Baby" together.*)

(*They finish the song and aerobicize themselves offstage.*)

*(The stage is bare for quite a while.)*

*(**JANE FONDA** escorts **RODNEY** and **OWEN** onstage, as though they were two dapper paramours. They are young and scruffy, your typical thirtysomething slackers. One is wearing a bonnet, the other a straw hat.)*

**OWEN.** Thank you, Jane.

**RODNEY.** Thank you, Jane.

*(They tip their hats to **JANE FONDA**. She nods and exits.)*

*(Lights change.)*

*(This scene is identical in tone to the previous hotel scene: fake, vivid, incredibly loud.)*

**RODNEY.** Where is she you fucking lost her / already.

**OWEN.** She was right behind you don't freak on me.

**RODNEY.** She's mine Owen.

**OWEN.** Where's the minibar…rock.

*(**OWEN** goes to the minifridge.)*

**RODNEY.** SHE'S MINE / OWEN

**OWEN.** Shhhh.

*(**RODNEY** tosses himself on the bed and begins bouncing.)*

**RODNEY.** This bed smells like starch and marinated ass…I like hotels I like hotels I like hotels.

**OWEN.** Okay, this is better. Feeling it now, feeling it. I'm here, The Rod is here, we are IN THE MOTHERFUCKIN' HIZZY. Now let's DO THIS THING.

*(**OWEN** cannot open the minibar.)*

**OWEN.** Locked? Jesus…

*(**AGNES** stumbles in behind them. She is red-faced and wears a gown and a sombrero.)*

**AGNES.** Wasted!

**RODNEY.** Wasted!

*(**AGNES** falls on the bed on top of **RODNEY**.)*

**AGNES.** This place is decent...

**RODNEY.** My uncle works for the chain.

*(They begin to kiss.)*

**OWEN.** Whoa. That feels really shitty, watching them do that. *(to **RODNEY**)* Hey. HEY. Hey RODNEY. Show her your new dance.

**RODNEY.** I made up a dance.

**AGNES.** Go on.

**RODNEY.** I don't have a name yet for it.

**AGNES.** Do they have whiskey?

**OWEN.** I can't get it open...

*(**OWEN** kicks the minibar furiously. It swings open. He begins rooting around inside.)*

**RODNEY.** You aren't watching...

**OWEN.** Go.

*(**RODNEY** does a complicated hip-hop move. **AGNES** applauds.)*

**OWEN.** He made it for Howard Stern.

**RODNEY.** Shut UP, dude.

*(**RODNEY** grabs **AGNES** by the hair. She does not react.)*

**OWEN.** He thinks if he can get on the air, he'll ask him to dance.

**RODNEY.** Most people think he's gross but he's got these ice blue eyes, that's why he wears sunglasses all the time.

*(**RODNEY** shoves **AGNES** onto the bed and presses his knee into her back, still holding her hair. He begins to tear off her clothes. She does not react. As a matter of fact, it seems to have a calming, pleasant effect on her.)*

*(**OWEN** pulls out a pack of cigarettes. He begins lighting them one by one and putting them out on **AGNES**'s body.)*

**RODNEY.** You're like psycho with that shit.

**OWEN.** For the blog...

**AGNES.** You guys aren't really brothers, are you...

**RODNEY.** We came out of the same womb...

**AGNES.** You're wild. You are wild.

**OWEN.** Are you two ready to kick it or will I stand here like a douche bag?

*(**RODNEY** begins to take off his bonnet.)*

**AGNES.** Leave the bonnet on.

*(**RODNEY** begins to tie **AGNES** up in the style of Abu Ghraib: he places a pillowcase over her head and attaches electric wires to her hands.)*

**RODNEY.** He's letting me have you first, he NEVER does that.

*(He shocks her five times. Each time, she lets out a shout of delight.)*

**OWEN.** Sweet. That's some subversive shit right there. That is CONTROVERSIAL. But that's the point, right? When you hit a nerve? POLARIZING. Some people just don't have the stomach for social commentary. They want butterflies and Bambi. Well fuck 'em. Right? Not my audience. I'm not the man with the lullaby, my friends. I'm the man with the MACHETE. A fugitive. Slicing down your tidy little forests. Everything that makes you feel safe? Shing. The lies you tell yourself? Shing. Truth to power. Burn it down, bitches.

**AGNES.** Come here...

**OWEN.** I'm fine.

**AGNES.** I paid for both...

**RODNEY.** Come on Owen...

**OWEN.** I'm thirsty...I'm going outside for a / Diet Coke

**AGNES.** Do not leave the fucking room.

*(Beat. **OWEN** reaches into his coat and pulls out a gun.)*

**AGNES.** Wait.

*(**OWEN** shoots **AGNES** in the face. Then he pulls a machete from his coat and hacks at her.)*

**OWEN.** Shing! Taste the blade! Skeeee-rumptious!

*(Then he pulls a sledgehammer from the closet and begins slamming it into her. Blood hits the wall.)*

**OWEN.** Rahg! World smells a whole lot better without your reeking hole…

*(He is finally done.)*

**OWEN.** Sweet Jesus that felt good.
**RODNEY.** GROSS.
**OWEN.** But maybe a little much.
**RODNEY.** Gross gross gross get her off me…

*(**OWEN** helps get **AGNES** off **RODNEY**. They roll her onto the floor.)*

**OWEN.** I may cut the sledgehammer.
**RODNEY.** You're kind of harsh sometimes. Get one for the blog.

*(**OWEN** poses with his cigarette in his mouth, one hand in a thumbs up, the other pointing to **AGNES**'s genitals.)*

**RODNEY.** Should I get in it, too?
**OWEN.** Yeah…pose a little.

*(**RODNEY** starts to remove the bonnet.)*

**OWEN.** Keep the fucking bonnet on.

*(**RODNEY** pretends to be raping **AGNES**'s body.)*

**OWEN.** Hoo-hoo! Beauteous.
**RODNEY.** I want a new dick, do you think we can buy me one?
**OWEN.** You don't need one anymore.
**RODNEY.** I may have quit raping but I still like my body to look slammin'…
**OWEN.** Make her talk.

*(lights change)*

*(**AGNES** pops up. She looks gorgeous, bloody and angelic in her gown.)*

*(**OWEN** looks at her longingly.)*

**AGNES.** *(slowly, seductively)* The table is set with gleaming silver, and everyone is wearing suits and gowns. I'm in one of those Academy Award jobbies, all long and shimmery. Everyone has just dined on pheasant and mints, and now they are sipping Turkish coffee. And then someone says, "Agnes, shall you play us a sonata?" And I say, "If you insist." And then I move toward the piano in my gown and place my long fingers on the keys, and I begin to play. And all the guests close their eyes and lean into one another. As though they have been dreaming of this moment.

*(**OWEN** inhales deeply, intoxicated.)*

**OWEN.** *(with longing)* I can smell your hair...

*(**AGNES** drops back down again.)*

**OWEN.** *(panic)* Agnes...

*(lights back to normal)*

**RODNEY.** You could have let me fuck her first, Owen. I was getting hard and everything...

**OWEN.** She's a lousy lay...

**RODNEY.** You can't tell by just looking at her.

**OWEN.** She's selfish. Comes too fast. And loud. And she's a liar.

**RODNEY.** How do you know?

**OWEN.** Lies and bullshit, every word. "I love you, Owen." Bullshit. "I've loved you since the day you screamed at me about the garage door." Bullshit. Look at her. SLUT SUPREME. Had more cock than a poultry farm. She can't play the piano worth shit. She has no class. She won't shut the fuck up. She's a cancer. She takes over your mind. You wanna tear your eyeballs out and feed them to the cat!

*(**JANE FONDA** enters and begins doing aerobics frantically.)*

**JANE FONDA.** You're losing it, Owen...

**OWEN.** She takes over, Jane. She eats my mind. I can smell her.

**JANE FONDA.** It's still early…you have time…

**OWEN.** I'm lost.

   *(sudden darkness)*

   *(a pause)*

   *(All we hear are two voices. We see nothing.)*

**AGNES'S VOICE.** Owen? Are you crying?

**OWEN'S VOICE.** I have a cold.

**AGNES'S VOICE.** I wanna talk to you…

**OWEN'S VOICE.** I need to finish this, Agnes.

**AGNES'S VOICE.** Remember when we were kids and I rode my garage door to the top and let go and fell on the asphalt sideways and broke my leg, and you wouldn't stop screaming at me?

**OWEN'S VOICE.** Yeah…

**AGNES'S VOICE.** And remember last week I went from zero to psycho when that dude honked at me for pulling out too far and so I double flipped him off and made a retarded fuck-you face and you were shocked?

**OWEN'S VOICE.** Kind of…

**AGNES'S VOICE.** And remember when you stepped on my finger and I tried to fake-cry to make you feel bad but it didn't work?

**OWEN'S VOICE.** No.

**AGNES'S VOICE.** I was just thinking about all that, all at once. I don't know why. And when I think like that, my inner crazy comes out and I want to hit you for like, I don't know. Loving me too much.

**OWEN'S VOICE.** You shouldn't hit me, Agnes.

**AGNES'S VOICE.** I know.

**OWEN'S VOICE.** You should never hit me.

**AGNES'S VOICE.** Because it emasculates you.

**OWEN'S VOICE.** Because it is tedious and it's UGLY.

*(Sound of hitting.* **AGNES** *giggles. More hitting.)*

**OWEN'S VOICE.** Stop it.

**AGNES'S VOICE.** You love me.

**OWEN'S VOICE.** STOP. IT.

**AGNES'S VOICE.** You love me, Owen.

**OWEN'S VOICE.** I'm trying to work.

**AGNES'S VOICE.** You love me too much.

**OWEN'S VOICE.** Why do you have to say it like that?

*(sound of a gun being cocked)*

**OWEN'S VOICE.** Where the fuck did you get that?

**AGNES'S VOICE.** It's mine…

**OWEN'S VOICE.** Put it down, Agnes…

**AGNES'S VOICE.** I like holding it. Makes me feel like a badass.

**OWEN'S VOICE.** Put it DOWN…

**AGNES'S VOICE.** I like it when you're scared of me. I feel like I can do anything. *(beat)* You're not gonna cry, are you? Like a little bitch?

**OWEN'S VOICE.** *(breaking)* Agnes…

**AGNES'S VOICE.** Why don't you go put on a dress, faggot?

**OWEN'S VOICE.** *(losing it)* I can't do this. I can't / do this.

**AGNES'S VOICE.** YOU ARE A GAYWAD! A WAD OF GAY! Turd licker. Ass muncher.

**OWEN'S VOICE.** I CAN'T DO THIS!

**AGNES'S VOICE.** THEN TRY HARDER!

*(lights change suddenly)*

*(We are in the dining hall of a very fancy room. A long table with a fine linen tablecloth is in the center of the room. The table is set for four, and on silver platters is a sumptuous spread of strange foods.)*

*(****AGNES*** *is rolling on the floor in a gown.* ***OWEN*** *is wearing a suit and has a gunshot wound in his head. He and* ***VALERIE*** *are seated at the table, waiting to eat. They are hungry and anxious, but it appears they are*

*waiting until the others get to the table before they start. They refuse to look at each other.)*

*(Finally, **RODNEY** emerges in a suit, sits at the table and dabs his mouth with a napkin. He snaps his fingers and **AGNES** stops rolling. She seats herself at the table.)*

*(**RODNEY** clasps his hands and the others follow suit. They all mumble the following at slightly different speeds:)*

**ALL.** Bless us oh Lord and these thy gifts which we are about to receive from your bountiful hands through Christ our Lord amen.

*(They cross themselves and begin to eat. They eat politely, tensely, occasionally glancing at one another, passing the wine, the grated cheese, the bread. They eat for a very long, tense time.)*

*(**VALERIE** can't take the tension any longer. She drops to the ground and begins rolling. After a moment, **RODNEY**, irritated, snaps his fingers. **VALERIE** sullenly returns to her seat.)*

*(They continue to eat, passing the gravy, the pepper, the peas.)*

*(After a long while, **AGNES** speaks to **OWEN**. Tonally, this should resemble a British drawing room comedy – stiff and strange (sans accents).)*

**AGNES.** What's that on your head?

*(**VALERIE** giggles. **OWEN** looks irritated. **RODNEY** ignores them.)*

*(They continue to eat in silence for a long time.)*

**RODNEY.** *(to **VALERIE**)* I think there's something wrong with you.

**VALERIE.** What?

**RODNEY.** The way you eat.

**VALERIE.** Oh.

*(Long silence. **VALERIE** tries to change the way she eats.)*

(JANE FONDA *appears and whips out a large pepper grinder.*)

**JANE FONDA.** Black pepper?

**RODNEY.** Black pepper.

(JANE FONDA *grinds.*)

**JANE FONDA.** Black pepper?

**OWEN.** Black pepper.

(JANE FONDA *grinds.*)

**RODNEY.** Thank you, Jane.

**OWEN.** Thank you, Jane.

(JANE FONDA, *frank and dignified, disappears.*)

**RODNEY.** She's so frank and dignified.

**OWEN.** I know.

**RODNEY.** I wish all women were like her.

*(Long silence. People eating.)*

(AGNES *is about to drink from her wine glass.*)

**OWEN.** You drink too much.

(AGNES *puts her wine glass back on the table without sipping.*)

**OWEN.** Don't fidget.

**AGNES.** I'm not.

**OWEN.** You're about to.

(AGNES *does not fidget.*)

*(Long silence. People eating and drinking.)*

(VALERIE *reaches for the bread.* RODNEY *slaps her hand away.*)

**AGNES.** Would anyone like me to play the piano?

**OWEN.** You can't fucking play the piano.

*(Long silence. People eating and drinking.)*

*(Suddenly,* RODNEY *pushes back in his chair and begins to shout the following;)*

**RODNEY.** SAY. I HAVE A FUNNY STORY!

*(The others exclaim: "Really?" "Bravo!" "Fantastic, go on!")*

**RODNEY.** It's rather comical. I think you'll enjoy it. It's about the time I nearly lost all my money!

*(More exclamations: "My word!" "You don't say!")*

**RODNEY.** It's a completely true story. I really think you'll enjoy it. I was in the war!

*(More exclamations.)*

**OWEN.** Which war?

**RODNEY.** THE war. The one I was in! I was in the war. And we were in this country. And there were several of us. Old Eddie and old Ronnie and old Johnnie and old Billy and old Charlie and old Artie and old Howie and old Rudy and old Jimmy and old Gary. And there was a cave. And the cave had two entrances. And we were chasing two guys. Two poop-flingers. We called them poop-flingers.

**OWEN.** Ha!

**RODNEY.** We called them poop-flingers because after they shat they wiped their asses with their hands and then flung their shit at the walls.

*(Exclamations: "No!" "They didn't!" "Disgusting!")*

And THEN they shook your hand.

*(More exclamations of disgust.)*

*(old war tale)* So we were chasing these two poop-flingers across this prairie, well it wasn't a prairie but it was a stretch of land not unlike a prairie except there were no prairie dogs, and then the land became rocks and the rocks turned into caves, and we were still chasing, and we weren't shooting because we knew about these caves and we knew the poop-flingers were running straight into the caves, and so we just chased them for a bunch of miles, and we lost sight of them because they were pretty fast, but then old Jimmy said he saw one

of them disappear into the cave with two entrances, and so old Eddie and old Ronnie and old Johnnie and old Billy climbed over the rocks to the other side of the cave, and we waited for their signal, and when they were in position old Eddie screamed POOP-TUBE!!! And they ran into the cave screaming, and the poop-flinger inside freaked and started running out the other side, and me and Charlie and Artie and Howie and Rudy and Jimmy and Gary were standing there with flame-throwers, and so when the poop-flinger came at us we torched him. But he was still running. And so we torched him again, and he kept running. He ran around in a little circle. And he was on fire. And his skin was melting off him. And there were screams, but they weren't his. There were other poop-flingers inside the poop-tube. They also came running out. They were on fire, too. They were much smaller than the first poop-flinger. Half his size. And one really small one.

(*long beat*)

**OWEN.** What happened to the prairie dogs?

**RODNEY.** There were none. I said that already.

**OWEN.** Right right, you did. My bad, sorry.

(*long beat*)

And so how did you lose your money?

**RODNEY.** When?

**OWEN.** You said, before your story. You said it was about nearly losing all your money.

**RODNEY.** Huh. I did, didn't I.

(*another long beat*)

(**RODNEY** *drinks from his wine glass.*)

**VALERIE.** Well I thought it was a marvelous story. Didn't you?

**AGNES.** Oh yes. I love stories. You are so funny. And your timing is spot on. You should be on stage.

**RODNEY.** No...

**AGNES.** You really should. You really should be on stage, telling stories. Like that fellow who drowned himself. You should be up there with a desk and a glass of water, telling funny little stories about your life.

**RODNEY.** I don't have the face for it.

**VALERIE.** Nonsense. You don't need a face. You don't even need a body. You just need your wits.

**RODNEY.** I'd have to think about it.

**VALERIE.** You really should.

**AGNES.** You really really should.

(**JANE FONDA** *enters again. She is carrying an enormous tray of Jell-O.*)

**OWEN.** Dessert! Excellent.

**RODNEY.** Ladies?

(**AGNES** *and* **VALERIE** *begin to clear the table, with the help of* **JANE FONDA**. *When they are done, they turn the table upside down and lay a plastic tarp on the underside.*)

(*Then* **AGNES** *and* **VALERIE** *take off their gowns. They are wearing lingerie underneath. They each do a line of coke off the other's ass.*)

(*Meanwhile,* **RODNEY** *and* **OWEN** *light up cigars. They sit perched forward in their chairs and begin to throw money down.*)

(**JANE FONDA** *dumps the Jell-O into the table.* **AGNES** *and* **VALERIE** *climb into the Jell-O table.* **JANE FONDA** *retrieves a whistle.*)

(**AGNES** *and* **VALERIE** *face-off.* **JANE FONDA** *blows the whistle.* **AGNES** *and* **VALERIE** *begin to wrestle in the Jell-O, as* **RODNEY** *and* **OWEN** *scream from the sidelines and chomp on their cigars, throwing down more money.*)

(*This goes on for quite a while; a full match. Someone wins. The winner of the betting collects his money.*)

*(Then **JANE FONDA** retrieves two feather pillows. She hands one to **AGNES** and one to **VALERIE**. She blows her whistle.)*

*(**AGNES** and **VALERIE** begin hitting each other with the pillows, giggling like little girls. **RODNEY** and **OWEN** watch, eating popcorn.)*

*(The pillows eventually explode into feathers and cover the girls. They giggle like crazy.)*

*(**RODNEY** and **OWEN** cheer.)*

*(After a moment, **VALERIE** becomes aggressive. She beats **AGNES** down with her pillow until **AGNES** is screaming in fear.)*

*(**VALERIE** exits.)*

*(**OWEN** regards **AGNES** in a puddle on the floor, Jell-O-ed and covered in feathers.)*

*(**RODNEY** pours his remaining popcorn onto **AGNES** and the floor. **OWEN** and **RODNEY** laugh and slap hands. **RODNEY** exits.)*

*(**JANE FONDA** begins to clean up the mess. **OWEN** looks sheepish.)*

**JANE FONDA.** Why are you doing this?

**OWEN.** I don't know.

**JANE FONDA.** Pathetic. Wipe that down. Jell-O everywhere. That was your dessert. I made it.

**OWEN.** I'm, I'm. She's just…arrrrgh. You know? I mean, how can I even/ try to

**JANE FONDA.** Shhht!

**OWEN.** This isn't easy for me.

**JANE FONDA.** Stand up.

*(**OWEN** stands. She approaches him.)*

**JANE FONDA.** The vigorous and sustained use of your entire imagination will not only tone the muscle of your mind, but will incinerate your worst memories and turn them into fuel. And what good are such toxic recollections if they cannot be converted to sustenance?

Hold out your hand.

(**JANE FONDA** *braces herself.*)

**JANE FONDA.** *(cont.)* I am she, now. The demon.

(**OWEN** *punches his hand, hard.* **JANE FONDA** *reacts as though she is being beaten.*)

The liar.

(**OWEN** *punches his hand.* **JANE FONDA** *reacts.*)

The bottomless eater.

(**OWEN** *punches his hand.* **JANE FONDA** *reacts.*)

The child.

(**OWEN** *punches his hand.* **JANE FONDA** *reacts.*)

The slut.

(**OWEN** *punches his hand.* **JANE FONDA** *reacts.*)

The cock-tease.

(**OWEN** *punches his hand.* **JANE FONDA** *reacts.*)

The vomitter.

(**OWEN** *punches his hand.* **JANE FONDA** *reacts.*)

The come-hitherer.

(**OWEN** *punches his hand.* **JANE FONDA** *reacts.*)

The make-you-cry-er.

(**OWEN** *punches his hand.* **JANE FONDA** *reacts.*)

The hair-sprayer.

(**OWEN** *punches his hand.* **JANE FONDA** *reacts.*)

The gown-wanter.

(**OWEN** *punches his hand.* **JANE FONDA** *reacts.*)

The makeup wearer.

(**OWEN** *punches his hand.* **JANE FONDA** *reacts.*)

**JANE FONDA.** *(cont.)* The use-all-the-hot-water-er.

(OWEN *punches his hand.* JANE FONDA *reacts.*)

The won't-shut-up-er.

(OWEN *punches his hand.* JANE FONDA *reacts.*)

The cheater.

(OWEN *punches his hand.* JANE FONDA *finally falls.*)

**OWEN.** Are you okay?

**JANE FONDA.** *(with dignity and grace)* Of course. It's my job.

(JANE FONDA *hands* OWEN *a gown, identical to the one* AGNES *wore.*)

**OWEN.** Thank you, Jane…

(JANE FONDA *stands and aerobicizes offstage.*)

(OWEN *steps into the gown.*)

Come on, Owen. Get into it. SLUT SUPREME.

*(He opens a makeup bag and begins applying makeup, facing forward.)*

I am so fucking pretty. I am so fucking fucking pretty, yo. Suckas. You wanna suck lemons from my cheeks. I got fuckin' mad pretty on my shit. My pretty is like PROFOUND. It has emissions. Waves of pretty. I'm like a gas burner of pretty. Stick a pot on me I'll make it whistle. Step the fuck off, right, 'cause my pretty will eat your soul. My pretty is a black hole. I am so pretty I drain all the ugly off you and wear it like a swimsuit. GODDAMN AM I PRETTY. Holy fucking shit. You can't stand it. You are like, she is so pretty I need to BASH her. I need to tear her pubes out. I need to hate on her. That pretty is cancerous. That pretty is a little iced cookie and I need to bite it. That pretty is TOXIC. That pretty boils in my gut, it eats me up, that pretty comes to me at night and scrapes all my tender spots. Soils my boxer briefs. That pretty is FUCKED-UP, I need to poke through it with my thumbs, I need to fuck the joy out of that pretty.

**OWEN.** *(cont.)* I want to kill that pretty. I want to kill that pretty. I want to kill that pretty.

*That's* what they say about me.

(**JANE FONDA** *enters. She yanks back a curtain to reveal...*)

(**RODNEY** *in rocker tights, big hair and eyeliner. He is pure rock 'n' roll.*)

(*Lights and music change.*)

(*We are in a rock 'n' roll video circa 1986...smoke, lights, etc. Whitesnake's "Still of the Night" blasts.* **RODNEY** *lip-synchs.\**)

(**OWEN** *becomes disturbed. Everything stops.*)

(*Both men face forward for the scene's duration.*)

(**RODNEY** *is miked. His voice is seductive, intimate.*)

**RODNEY.** What's the matter, Owen?

**OWEN.** I feel strange.

**RODNEY.** About what?

**OWEN.** I don't know.

**RODNEY.** Can I do something?

**OWEN.** Hit me in the face. Get me angry, get me all riled up.

**RODNEY.** Fist or palm?

**OWEN.** Fist. No, palm.

(**OWEN** *closes his eyes. He waits. He reacts as though he is being kissed very passionately on the lips – but this should be genuine.*)

(**RODNEY** *does as well.*)

(**OWEN** *opens his eyes.*)

Again.

(**OWEN** *closes his eyes again, and reacts similarly, as does* **RODNEY.**)

(**OWEN** *opens his eyes.*)

Try to get your tongue into it.

\*See Music Use Note on page 3.

*(OWEN closes his eyes again, and reacts in muted delight.)*

*(He opens his eyes.)*

**OWEN.** Am I blushing?

**RODNEY.** Yes.

**OWEN.** One more.

*(another kiss)*

**OWEN.** Okay.

**RODNEY.** You happy?

**OWEN.** Yeah.

**RODNEY.** Jubilant?

**OWEN.** Yeah, yeah. Thanks. I love you baby. I love you. I love you so much. I want to have a baby. Can we have a baby? I want a baby that looks like you. I want him to have your funny little nose, your eyelashes. I want to make a person who is a product of our love. Can we do that, baby?

**RODNEY.** Sure.

**OWEN.** Thank you baby. I love you. I love us.

**RODNEY.** Sweet.

*(**RODNEY** tumbles offstage. **OWEN** goes into labor.)*

**OWEN.** Jane…my water broke…

*(**JANE FONDA** rushes in.)*

**JANE FONDA.** Okay, just breathe with me, and two and breathe, and two and push, and two and breathe…

**OWEN.** It hurts…

**JANE FONDA.** …and two and again…oh, I can see the head…okay now push, Owen! Push!

**OWEN.** It hurts, Jane…

**JANE FONDA.** Come on! You can do it! PUSH!

**OWEN.** Raaarrgghhhh!!!

*(**OWEN** gives birth. **JANE FONDA** hands the baby to him.)*

(**OWEN** *places the baby to his nipple and nurses the baby in exhausted, blissed-out motherhood.*)

**JANE FONDA.** Well done, Owen! Aw, look at you. You're a mother! You must be over the moon.

**OWEN.** I couldn't have done it without you, Jane.

**JANE FONDA.** How are you feeling?

**OWEN.** Really good.

**JANE FONDA.** I'm so proud of you. I think you're finally ready.

**OWEN.** Awesome.

**JANE FONDA.** Go to it!

(**JANE FONDA** *begins aerobicizing once again.*)

(*Lights up on the hotel room again.*)

(**RODNEY**, *back in normal slacker gear, is reading the newspaper and drinking seltzer.*)

(*Unlike the previous hotel scenes, this room feels authentic and hyper-real. The acting is naturalized.*)

(**OWEN** *sits at his computer and begins typing furiously.*)

(**JANE FONDA** *enters the hotel room.*)

**JANE FONDA.** To get the full benefit from the workout you must do it with me from beginning to end without stopping.

(**JANE FONDA** *enters the TV. A workout video on-screen picks up where she left off.*)

**OWEN.** *(regarding his typing)* Yes yes yes…smack that juicy groove…

**JANE FONDA'S VOICE.** It is this vigorous and sustained use of your entire body that will not only tone your muscles but will burn up calories, and improve your circulation.

(**RODNEY** *mutes the volume on the workout video.*)

**RODNEY.** *(regarding the newspaper)* Holy shit. They found that guy. The one that blew up that clinic in Atlanta.

**OWEN.** *(not listening)* Oh?

**RODNEY.** They found all this shit on him. Gasoline cans, flares, starter fluid, propane tanks and a pistol. He was on his way to do another.

**OWEN.** Huh.

**RODNEY.** Unless those chicks got to him first.

**OWEN.** Right.

**RODNEY.** I'd like to fuck them.

**OWEN.** Huh.

**RODNEY.** I'd like to fuck them both at once. Put one on each side, then do like a flip and poke. *(demonstrating)* Flip, poke, flip, poke. Right? Pump my jiz right in their snatches. Knock 'em both up, then I'll be all, "Abort THAT, bitches…" I mean what's their fucking deal, right?

**OWEN.** Their sister got blown up, dude.

**RODNEY.** How do you know, dude?

**OWEN.** It's on their blog.

**RODNEY.** Hey did you know one of them is a dyke? I'm like, "Figures."

*(**RODNEY** is bored. He bends over and sniffs the blanket on his bed.)*

**RODNEY.** Dude, this place is decent.

**OWEN.** My uncle works for the chain.

**RODNEY.** Could get used to this shit. Too bad I'm only on leave for a week.

*(**OWEN** continues typing. **RODNEY** continues reading the newspaper. He's bored. He does some aerobics.)*

**RODNEY.** You hungry?

**OWEN.** Yeah.

**RODNEY.** I'm fuckin' hungry, dude.

*(**RODNEY** picks up the phone and dials.)*

**RODNEY.** Hi. We'd like some room service please. Eggs benedict, and could you substitute the homefries with like fruit? I dunno, apples, strawberries...and send up some coffee and like a, do you have anything chocolate? Okay, that too...Owen, what do you want?

**OWEN.** Do they have Chex?

**RODNEY.** Do you have Chex? *(to* **OWEN***)* Raisin Bran and Rice Krispies and granola.

**OWEN.** Grilled cheese then. With tomatoes and mustard.

**RODNEY.** Grilled cheese with tomatoes and mustard. Thanks, dude.

*(He hangs up. He's bored.)*

**RODNEY.** Do they get Howard Stern out here?

**OWEN.** You need Satellite to get him.

**RODNEY.** Most people think he's gross but dude, he's got these, like, ice blue eyes. That's why he wears sunglasses all the time.

*(He is bored again. He sniffs the blanket again.)*

**RODNEY.** Fabric softener.

*(****RODNEY*** *is still bored.)*

**RODNEY.** I should piss the bed. Dare me?

*(****RODNEY*** *jumps on the bed and drops his pants.)*

**RODNEY.** Dare me, quick! 'Cause even if you don't I'll still do it...

**OWEN.** I dare you.

*(****RODNEY*** *tries to pee.* ***OWEN*** *watches him.* ***RODNEY*** *notices him watching.* ***OWEN*** *looks away.)*

**RODNEY.** Pee, pee...Ssssss...argh, performance anxiety!!! Wait...there's a trickle...

*(****RODNEY*** *pees on the bed.)*

**RODNEY.** I'M PEEING IN THE BED! I'M PEEING IN THE BED! HOW FUCKING AWESOME IS THAT?

**OWEN.** Completely. Dude, please let me finish this, I'm almost done.

*(****RODNEY*** *finishes peeing on the bed. He zips up and becomes immediately bored.)*

*(He un-mutes the **JANE FONDA** video.)*

**JANE FONDA'S VOICE.** Head right, two and back, two, and side, two, and front, stretch it out and to the right, two and reverse, two…

**RODNEY.** Man. She's so fucking PERT. Does she tie that on every morning or did she grow that way?

**OWEN.** Pause it for a second.

*(**RODNEY** pauses the TV.)*

**RODNEY.** What?

**OWEN.** SHUT THE FUCK UP? PLEASE? (a) You see me working here, (b) this room is going to smell like piss all night, (c) you promised you would let me fucking work if I brought you here and (d) you sound retarded.

*(Beat. **RODNEY** smacks the back of **OWEN**'s head.)*

**OWEN.** Don't hit me, man.

*(**RODNEY** smacks the back of **OWEN**'s head again.)*

**OWEN.** Don't do it again.

*(He does it again.)*

*(They scuffle, wrestle, etc., hurling each other playfully around the room.)*

**OWEN.** Fucker…

**RODNEY.** Pussy…

*(**RODNEY** accidentally slips off the bed and slams his face against something hard.)*

**OWEN.** Whoa. You okay man?

**RODNEY.** Think so.

*(**RODNEY** feels the inside of his mouth with his tongue.)*

**OWEN.** Are you bleeding?

**RODNEY.** Little.

**OWEN.** Lemme see.

*(**OWEN** checks the inside of **RODNEY**'s mouth.)*

**OWEN.** You got cut on your tooth.

(**OWEN** *takes a piece of ice from the bucket and ices the inside of* **RODNEY**'s *cheek.*)

**RODNEY.** Cold!

**OWEN.** Don't move.

(**OWEN** *grabs a tissue and blots the inside of* **RODNEY**'s *cheek. Then* **OWEN** *hands* **RODNEY** *the mouthwash.*)

**OWEN.** Rinse, so it won't get infected.

(**RODNEY** *rinses.*)

**RODNEY.** Faggot.

**OWEN.** You're the faggot, faggot.

**RODNEY.** I beg to differ, my faggot.

**OWEN.** Who's the faggot who just whipped his dick out in front of me?

**RODNEY.** Who's the faggot with all the Jane Fonda tapes?

**OWEN.** That's RESEARCH, faggot.

(*There's a knock on the door.* **RODNEY** *opens the door.*)

(**JANE** *[not* **JANE FONDA***] stands with a cart of lidded silver platters.*)

**RODNEY.** Wheel it on in…

(**JANE** *wheels the cart into the room.*)

**RODNEY.** Sweetheart, this asshole just pissed in the bed. Could you send someone up to change the sheets?

**JANE.** Of course.

(**JANE** *removes the lid from the grilled cheese with a flourish.*)

**RODNEY.** Faaaaancyyyyyyy.

(**JANE** *removes the lid from the eggs benedict.*)

**RODNEY.** Oh yeah…

(**JANE** *pours coffee into two cups, holding the coffee pot very high.* **RODNEY** *is mesmerized.*)

**JANE.** Sugar?

**RODNEY.** Three for me, none for him.

(**JANE** *places three cubes into* **RODNEY***'s coffee.*)

**JANE.** Black pepper?

**RODNEY.** Black pepper….

(**JANE** *whips out a pepper grinder from nowhere and expertly grinds three times over the food. Then she hands him a cloth napkin.*)

**RODNEY.** You are really good at that. What's your name?

**JANE.** Jane.

**RODNEY.** Like Fonda!

**JANE.** Sure.

**RODNEY.** How long have you been working here, Jane?

**JANE.** About six months…

**RODNEY.** Do you like it?

**JANE.** I like it enough.

**RODNEY.** Do you get benefits and stuff?

**JANE.** The usual. Health, 401(k)…

**RODNEY.** I'll bet you see a lot of assholes…

**JANE.** Ah…

**RODNEY.** I'll bet you see a lot of rich fucking assholes who treat you like shit.

**JANE.** People are generally all right…

**RODNEY.** You're way polite, Jane. Do you get that a lot?

**JANE.** Once in a while.

**RODNEY.** I suppose you have to be or else you'd get raped a lot. Are you hungry? I probably won't eat all of this…

**JANE.** I ate, but thank you.

**RODNEY.** Would you come up later and change the sheets for us?

**JANE.** I can send up a maid…

**RODNEY.** No, you should come. We want you.

**JANE.** I don't generally make up the beds…

**RODNEY.** But you will, okay? Because I'm a fucking filthy rapist and I want to get you pregnant.

**JANE.** *(polite and vaguely flirtatious)* You kiss your mother with that mouth?

**RODNEY.** Only on her beef curtains…Come back in about twenty minutes. We'll be done eating by then, right Owen?

(**OWEN** *lets out a nervous a laugh.*)

**RODNEY.** And then you can hang out a little? Although we have no whiskey…could you bring some up?

**JANE.** I'll see what I can do.

**RODNEY.** Thanks Jane…

**JANE.** It's my job.

**RODNEY.** Bye.

(**JANE** *exits.* **RODNEY** *gleefully grabs his plate and sits on the bed.* **OWEN** *begins cracking up, but he's kind of scared. They slap hands.*)

**OWEN.** Hoooo!

**RODNEY.** Now THAT'S dignity.

(**RODNEY** *begins scarfing his food in huge bites.*)

**OWEN.** *(giddy and disturbed)* "Beef curtains…" Holy shit. You are fucking LECHEROUS, dude.

**RODNEY.** The Rod is in the hizzy! Fuck this is good. Come eat. I hate eating alone. Makes me feel like an addict. That's a good line. You should put it in your screenplay.

**OWEN.** Taking it all in…

(**OWEN** *types.* **RODNEY** *eats.*)

*(beat)*

**RODNEY.** Must be nice. To have a calling.

**OWEN.** You have a calling.

**RODNEY.** Any fucker with a rifle and conscience could do what I do.

**OWEN.** I couldn't.

**RODNEY.** What's it about?

OWEN. Uhhh…it's like a "based on." Like "based on a true story."

RODNEY. Like, autobiographical?

OWEN. Uh. Yeah, sorta. But also I'm taking shit from like, the news.

RODNEY. Like what shit?

OWEN. The abortion chicks.

RODNEY. The ones with the blog?

(OWEN *nods.*)

RODNEY. OUTRAGEOUS! Hello, Maestro!

OWEN. Research.

RODNEY. HELLO, Maestro!

OWEN. But it's fictionalized…I don't want to get sued.

RODNEY. Pitch it to me.

OWEN. Well, it's early, but…and also it might change…

RODNEY. "I got Shpeilberg at two, don't have all day…"

OWEN. Okay. So like, there's the two chicks. They're like sisters. Or half sisters. They tell everyone that. And they are SO FUCKING HOT.

RODNEY. Right?

OWEN. So hot that like, your eyebrows get singed around them. Like too hot. And rude. So rude that you like have to put them into a condom. I mean they are SICK. Heavy shit, these two. And one is a bulimic.

RODNEY. Sick.

OWEN. SO sick. And the other is. I dunno. Puerto Rican or something. A real bulldog. Smart, ballsy. Doesn't take shit.

RODNEY. But they're sisters. And they make out occasionally.

OWEN. Yeah, 'cause like one's a secret lezzy.

RODNEY. The PR.

OWEN. Yeah. AND, she's been fucking the bulimic's husband since they were sixteen.

RODNEY. Right.

**OWEN.** And they do coke off each other's asses in front of some businessmen. At a dinner party. They're strippers. EX-strippers.

**RODNEY.** You should make the PR girl blind.

**OWEN.** Why?

**RODNEY.** And make it like she got fucked over by the two businessmen, which is why she hates men so bad.

**OWEN.** Which is why she's fucking her sister's husband. Because she secretly hates him, too.

**RODNEY.** But he's really not a bad guy.

**OWEN.** No. He's just. He has a back problem and a bowel problem. He has to wear a diaper. He fucks her because (a) she's SICK hot, and (b) he feels bad for her. Because she has jaundice.

**RODNEY.** She's blind AND has jaundice?

**OWEN.** Ho, wait. Hepatitis, not jaundice. I get them confused.

**RODNEY.** Everyone does.

**OWEN.** So like, then she accuses the husband of raping her, which is how the bulimic finds out they were fucking.

**RODNEY.** But he didn't rape her.

**OWEN.** Nah, dude. There was no fucking rape. YET. But like, okay, so here's the meat:
one night PR is on the pole, right? And she's workin' it. Good night, bachelor party up front, Japanese suits in the back…In walks Bulimia. And Bulimia's got this LOOK on her face, like a little…

(**OWEN** *trembles his bottom lip.*)

**RODNEY.** The trembly lip! HATE that shit.

**OWEN.** *(girl voice)* "Our baby sister got capped," she says. "Some neo-con stuffed his trunk full of shit and drove up outside this clinic. BOOOOM. They found part of her hanging from a telephone pole three blocks away."

**RODNEY.** The armpit…

**OWEN.** What? No man, like a, like a shoe or. But so they stand there, and they DON'T EVEN CRY. No crying.

Not even a whimper. DIGNITY SUPREME. The PR just kind of turns to the camera and looks us dead in the eye and says, "IT'S ON."

**RODNEY.** It *is* on.

**OWEN.** So PR's like the mastermind of the whole enterprise. She (a) makes the blog, (b) gets the camera and (c) buys the gun. She writes this long-ass manifesto – all this shit about her uterus, the internet, the FCC, etc. They pool all their stripper money together and procure a hoopty. They motor from state to state and show up to all these pro-life conventions looking like Grade A Tail. They bring home the sloppy dudes. Fuck 'em if they can get wood. And THEN.

(**OWEN** *makes gun-fingers and pulls the trigger.*)

**OWEN.** BANG! *(girl voice)* "Keep your laws off my fucking body!!"

**RODNEY.** Fucking CHILLING, man. There's a market for that shit.

**OWEN.** There's TOTALLY a market for this shit! These bitches with the blog, they're like female Dukes of Hazzard. Taking the law into their own hands. *(girl voice)* "Don't fuck with me suckas or I will cut you!"

**RODNEY.** Dude. There's your title.

**OWEN.** I already have a title. *(marquee title)* An Unbearable Proposition.

**RODNEY.** I like it. I like it.

**OWEN.** And there's more! So one night they're in Mississippi at this convention. Everything is swell. Dude's getting sloppy, spilling Wild Turkey on his pants. They make the transaction. PR goes to her car to get change. Dude follows her out and BEATS THE LIVING CRAP OUT OF HER. I mean she is TOTALLY fucked-up. Black eye, lip hanging. But of course she looks so fucking hot. So she's there in the hospital, all fucked-up and hot. And THEN there's rape. Lots of it. The orderly rapes the PR. And then the doctor. And then a male nurse. It's one big bang-fest. And the dudes feel fucking AWFUL about it. But the PR lezzy NEVER FUCKING CRIES. She stands all shaky and bloody and dignified with her chin turned up, and then the doctor who was the last to have her –

**RODNEY.** A neurosurgeon!

**OWEN.** He can't look her in the face, because this is like his greatest downfall, he's like "Tragically Flawed Dude," hubris and all that, he's like Hamlet, right, and he thinks about how in med school they never prepared you for the fuckable lost ones, you know the ones who don't actually look into your eyes but through you as if you were a pile of ash because of all the fucked-up ruinous shit from their past, a molesty step-dad or white slavery or whatever, so they gotta exact some foul revenge on you because you are (a) in the way and (b) looking like someone who needs to be taken down, and so they spread their damage on a shiny silver platter and say, "Munch it, baby," and you just can't stop yourself because nothing tastes more delicious than a steaming hot mound of damage.

So the doctor is thinking this shit, and then he thinks of his wife at home and his two sons, they're twins and they wear matching baseball pajamas to bed, and his wife lost all the baby weight the second they popped out because she didn't want to be one of those lard–asses in the Key Foods wearing sweatpants and a hairnet, and like she never leaves the house without makeup, and all his golf buddies are like, "How the fuck did YOU land such a tasty beverage," and he gets fake-mad at them but he is secretly so fucking proud because he's the only one of them who still gets regular blowjobs, and when he goes home that night she'll be waiting for him on the porch drinking a glass of white wine and smoking a jay, and she'll offer him a hit and ask him how his day was, and at that moment – AT THAT MOMENT – he'll conjure that bloody fucking broken cunty bitch in her little hospital gown and her eyes made of ash and he will release her into the evening air and she will never enter his mind again.

**OWEN.** *(cont.)* So this neurosurgeon is finishing up his rape, and he's pulling up his scrubs and thinking about his wife and not looking at PR, and PR tries to say something all significant like a supreme like philosophical sentence or whatever, but he whispers, "Just go." And walks out. And she's left there alone in the room. And she stands up all wobbly on her colt legs, and her hospital gown is all open and you can see her titties –

**RODNEY.** And her bush! NC-17...

**OWEN.** And then Bulimia shows up. And she looks at PR, all fucked-up and raped. And she's like, wait a second. I'm still sore about PR fucking my husband. But what she DOESN'T know is – get this – is that PR fucked her husband to get the cizash for their baby sister's abortion!

**RODNEY.** Joan of Arc!

**OWEN.** And Bulimia DOESN'T KNOW! So Bulimia steps out of the room to quote unquote "get a Diet Coke," and comes back with a gat. BAM.

**RODNEY.** Right in the face.

**OWEN.** Never saw her coming.

**RODNEY.** Blind motherfucking whore.

**OWEN.** Um wait. She's not blind. She's just normal.

*(He types a little.)*

**OWEN.** And dykey. A little dykey.

**RODNEY.** Not man-dykey...

**OWEN.** No, normal. Wears dresses and thongs but likes to fuck girls.

**RODNEY.** It's so topical.

**OWEN.** Right? Some fucked-up shit chicks go through. Rape and babies and stripping, and being objectified by the media...

*(small beat)*

**RODNEY.** Are you like a FEMINIST?

**OWEN.** *(genuine)* I want to write a movie my mom will be proud of. My mom is a strong fucking woman, homes. Every time one of her ex-husbands dumps on her, she takes it like a pro. Chin up. Pure class. Tablecloths and linens. That's my mom.

**RODNEY.** Right on.

**OWEN.** She's my hero, man. And you know who her hero is?

**RODNEY.** No clue.

**OWEN.** *(points to TV)* Hanoi. Fucking. Jane.

**RODNEY.** *(delighted)* Traitorous commie bitch. Full circle, dude!

**OWEN.** Precision!

**RODNEY.** Minty fresh! That's beautiful.

**OWEN.** Yeah? You weren't bored or anything?

**RODNEY.** Yeah, a little. Yo, I heard she did threesomes with her French husband. AGAINST HER WILL.

**OWEN.** How do you force someone to do a threesome?

**RODNEY.** She didn't WANT to, but she loved him so much she did it anyway. That's one special female.

**OWEN.** Dignity, man. "Don't fuck with me. I'll do what you want, but don't fuck with me." It's about self-respect.

**RODNEY.** Right. "How can I respect you when you don't respect yourself?"

**OWEN.** Exactly. *(beat)* I'm glad you're here, man.

**RODNEY.** Me, too. Want your grilled cheese?

**OWEN.** I'm starving.

*(Beat. OWEN eats.)*

**OWEN.** Yo. I'm thinking about putting the war in my screenplay.

**RODNEY.** Yeah?

**OWEN.** I wanna juxtapose the crap in the Middle East with the war on women's bodies. Not sure how yet. It's an experiment.

**RODNEY.** You should put in that fucked-up shit I told you.

**OWEN.** I did.

(*beat*)

**RODNEY.** You did? About the thirteen-year-old chick?

**OWEN.** No, man. The other shit. The cave with two entrances. Poop-tube.

**RODNEY.** Oh. (*beat*) You should put in the other thing, too.

**OWEN.** The…the…

**RODNEY.** Because it was fucked-up. And no one's talking about it.

**OWEN.** Man, I / don't

**RODNEY.** (*quietly*) All of us, man. One after another. She just laid there. Never cried, not once. Then we shoved a grenade in her snatch. Pulled the fucking pin. (*long beat*) Who's gonna tell the tales? You, man. (*long beat*) Because I'm dyslexic.

**OWEN.** I'll think about it.

**RODNEY.** That's all I ask. (*beat*) Am I in it?

**OWEN.** Um…kinda…

**RODNEY.** Damn! Academy Awards! Roll up in the Bentley, be all, "S'up, Betties, it's The Rod"…do I get to hump anyone?

**OWEN.** A corpse.

**RODNEY.** Whoa. I don't like that.

**OWEN.** But it isn't really you, dude. Like I'll be working it, trying to make the females into human beings, and then I'll fucking lose it. So I stick us in there for a while until I get it back.

**RODNEY.** Does it work?

**OWEN.** Fuck, yeah!

**RODNEY.** Process. I like it. Using models. You're an artist. I never knew any artists. Faggot.

**OWEN.** Suck me.

**RODNEY.** Who's the bulimic?

(**OWEN** *says nothing.*)

**RODNEY.** Not Agnes.

> (**OWEN** *says nothing.*)

That ratty piece of neighborhood trash?

> (**OWEN** *says nothing.*)

That's cool, that's cool. She's like your muse.

**OWEN.** Whatever.

> (**OWEN** *finishes his sandwich.* **RODNEY** *slaps him on the back.*)

**RODNEY.** Yo. You are WRITING THAT SHIT. GO WRITE THAT SHIT, man.

**OWEN.** Fo' shizzle.

> (**OWEN** *returns to typing.* **RODNEY** *returns to the* **JANE FONDA** *video.*)

**OWEN.** Turn it up. I wanna hear her.

**RODNEY.** Inspiration. Riiiiight. Hello, Maestro!

**OWEN.** Hell-LO!

> (**RODNEY** *turns up the volume.* **OWEN** *types.*)
>
> (*lights change*)
>
> (**JANE FONDA** *appears, dressed in her Hanoi Jane gear.*)
>
> (**OWEN** *remains on stage, typing throughout. He mouths the words that the girls shout, getting more and more excited by the minute.*)

**JANE FONDA.** Men.

You think you can do whatever you want with me, think again.

You think that I'm so delicate?

You think you have to care for me?

You throw me to the ground.

You think I break?

> (**JANE FONDA** *throws herself to the ground, aerobic-style.*)

You think I can't get up again? You think I can't get up again?

(**JANE FONDA** *gets up.*)

**JANE FONDA.** You think I need a man to save my life?

*(She throws herself to the ground again.)*

I don't need a man! I don't need a man!

*(She gets up, does some aerobics and throws herself to the ground again and again as she yells.)*

*(***OWEN*** types.)*

These men can fuck themselves!
These men are leeches.
These men are cheaters.
These rapists,
these politicians,
these war mongers.

*(She throws herself to the ground over and over.)*

*(Music kicks in over this – maybe a techno version of J. S. Bach's "Sleepers Awake!" from Cantata No. 140 [although I'm sure there's a better and more appropriate song choice out there], and as she hits the ground over and over, repeating her same litany as she does, **AGNES** and **VALERIE** enter, wearing military fatigues. They watch her.)*

*(***AGNES*** joins in, and starts throwing herself to the ground aerobically and synchronously so that it is a choreographed aerobics piece of the two women.)*

*(***VALERIE*** watches. ***OWEN*** types.)*

**JANE FONDA & AGNES.**
These faggots,
these soldiers,
these impregnators,
these golfers,
neo-cons,
neuro surgeons,
screenplay writers!

*(Now **AGNES** starts to yell, too, simultaneously with **JANE FONDA**, on top of her words, as both of them continue to throw themselves to the ground over and over.)*

*(**OWEN** types.)*

| **JANE FONDA.** | **AGNES.** |
|---|---|
| These men should be eliminated! | These men! |
| These men should be snuffed out! | These men! |
| Who needs a man? | All I wanted was a man who could be a man |
| Who needs a man? | a man who wouldn't cry |
| I'll make it on my own. | a man who would let me drin |
| I'm an autonomous person! | a man who would fight for m' honor |
| I'm an independent person! | And I don't think it's wrong |
| I am frank and dignified! | to drink a little sometimes |
| I can do what I want! | and wear perfume |
| I can be who I am! | and keep myself skinny |
| And I can also be who you want me to be! | to like my clothes |
| Hey! | and think they're sexy |
| I don't actually want men to be eliminated! | and wear short skirts |
| I just said that so you will respect me! | that blow up in the wind |
| I'll say anything you want | I don't think it's wrong |
| And do anything you want | for several men to love me at once |
| Just so you'll respect me! | to like to touch me |
| | and listen to me |
| | and talk to me |
| | and write me notes |
| | and give me flowers |
| | because I like men |
| | I like men |
| | And, I like to be hit sometimes. |

*(And, finally, **VALERIE** joins in, too, until all three women are yelling their words over the loud music and throwing themselves to the ground over and over.)*

*(**OWEN** types.)*

**ALL THREE WOMEN TOGETHER.**
Why can't a man
be more like a woman?

**VALERIE.** *(Puerto Rican accent)*
I don't know what I'm doing here
I don't want a man to be more like a woman
I just want a woman.
Emotionally available
Able to process.
To deal with her feelings.
To speak from the heart
to say what she means.
To not violate me
To not violate me
To not violate me
Or hit me
Or shoot me in the face.

**AGNES.**
I don't want a man I can hit
I don't want a pussy.
I don't want a woman.

**JANE FONDA.**
I have self-respect
I have dignity
I want a woman
If you want me to have a woman

**ALL THREE WOMEN TOGETHER.**
I am not conflicted!
I know exactly who I am!
I know exactly what I want!

*(The women then tear their fatigues off and begin pole-dancing and rubbing up against each other.)*

*(**OWEN** stops typing a moment and watches, as...)*

*(**RODNEY** enters in army fatigues. He pulls out a rifle. He executes them, one by one.)*

*(Lights change to a soft flickering light. Bombs can be heard exploding outside.)*

*(A hospital room. **VALERIE** is lying in her bed, all beaten up in her hospital gown. She is the picture of dignity. Her chin is high.)*

*(This scene is heightened in the style of a sweeping wartime epic, underscored by music. This is **OWEN**'s film.)*

*(**AGNES** enters, dramatically. She wears a burka.)*

*(**VALERIE** has a Puerto Rican accent.)*

**VALERIE.** Oh hello, Nouri al-Maliki Mahmoud...have you come for my daily sponge bath?

**AGNES.** I am not Nouri al-Maliki Mahmoud...

**VALERIE.** Are you with the resistance?

**AGNES.** I was, once...a long long time ago...

**VALERIE.** Agnes? Could it be you?

*(A weighted pause. She whips off her burka.)*

**AGNES.** Yes.

*(**AGNES** embraces **VALERIE**. **VALERIE** winces in pain.)*

**AGNES.** Dear God, what have they done to you?

**VALERIE.** The boys here have been a little, how shall I say... overly friendly.

**AGNES.** They didn't. They wouldn't!

**VALERIE.** They have. Many times over.

**AGNES.** They will pay for this...

**VALERIE.** Oh Agnes...save your fury for the battlefield. So rarely do they see a kind face here, a kind soul. A kind heart. These are broken men, Agnes. Men who have lost their spirit. There is no one left to give them what they want, so they feel they must take it. Please don't blame them...blame the war.

**AGNES.** This infernal war!

*(A huge, shattering bomb explodes nearby. The women cover their heads. Pieces of plaster fall from the ceiling.)*

**VALERIE.** Oh Agnes…you must get out of here before it's too late…

**AGNES.** But what about you?

**VALERIE.** I know I won't get out alive. I've made my peace.

*(**AGNES** hurls herself onto the bed and begins to weep.)*

**VALERIE.** Don't cry for me, my dear sister…

**AGNES.** You don't understand…I came here to kill you…

*(Another huge bomb explodes outside. More plaster falls.)*

**VALERIE.** What do you mean?

**AGNES.** All those years you were sleeping with my husband…I swore I would get revenge…but then we formed the resistance…and I believed we were working toward something much bigger…but then the resistance fell apart…we are losing the war, Valerie…all around us is in ruins…nothing but despair and heartache…

**VALERIE.** Then do it, Agnes…kill me.

*(**AGNES** pulls out a gun. She holds it up to shoot **VALERIE**, her arm trembling.)*

**VALERIE.** *(supremely dignified)* Go on. Pull the trigger.

**AGNES.** I…can't…

*(She drops the gun and flees to **VALERIE**. They stare into each other's eyes a moment. They kiss passionately.)*

*(**OWEN** enters in a lab coat with a rolling tray of food.)*

*(**AGNES** scrambles to get her burka back on.)*

**AGNES.** Oh…

**OWEN.** Sorry for the interruption…

*(**OWEN** hands **VALERIE** a bedpan. She tucks it under herself and pees, all with great pain. Then she hands it back to **OWEN**.)*

**OWEN.** Lunch time.

*(**OWEN** uncovers a little plastic tray.)*

**AGNES.** Thank goodness. I'm starving.
**VALERIE.** But Agnes…you don't eat…
**AGNES.** *(hurt)* You don't know me any more, Valerie…

> (**OWEN** *uncovers another little plastic tray.*)

**AGNES.** Grilled cheese…
**OWEN.** With mustard.

> (**OWEN** *pours coffee into two cups, holding the coffee pot very high.* **AGNES** *is mesmerized.*)

**AGNES.** You are really good at that.
**VALERIE.** Agnes…

> (**AGNES** *ignores* **VALERIE** *and flirts mercilessly with* **OWEN**.)

> (**OWEN** *begins to sing "Pretty Baby" to himself as he pours.*)

**OWEN** *(singing)* Everybody loves a baby / That's why I'm in love with you / Pretty Baby, Pretty Baby.
Sugar?
**AGNES.** Three for me, none for her.
**VALERIE.** Agnes, please…

> (**OWEN** *places three cubes into* **AGNES***'s coffee.*)

**OWEN.** *(singing)* And I'd like to be your sister, brother / Dad and mother, too / Pretty Baby, Pretty Baby.

*(He whips out a paper napkin and hands it to her.)*

**AGNES.** What song is that?
**OWEN.** I don't know…my mother used to sing it to me.
**AGNES.** What's your name?
**OWEN.** Owen.
**AGNES.** I knew a fellow named Owen once…
**OWEN.** Did you.
**AGNES.** He was a bit of a pansy. He let me hit him. And he cried all the time. His penis was shaped like a cashew. He was in love with his best friend. He called him "The Rod." Isn't that hilarious?

*(A bruised **VALERIE** begins to leave the bed.)*

**VALERIE.** *(wounded)* I'm going outside for a Diet Coke…

*(**OWEN** suddenly grabs the gun that **AGNES** dropped earlier and aims it at **VALERIE**.)*

**OWEN.** Do not leave the fucking room.

**AGNES.** Oh my God…You're one of THEM…

**OWEN.** That's right, American gypsy…

*(He aims the gun at **AGNES** and grips **VALERIE** by her throat.)*

**OWEN.** You two ladies thought you could defeat us with your little "resistance." Well we've had you in our sights for a long time. And payback is a total bitch. *(to **AGNES**)* I advise you to watch carefully, Agnes. *(to **VALERIE**)* I'm going to rape you now, Valerie.

*(**VALERIE** nods. With dignity, she leans back and spreads her legs.)*

**AGNES.** NOOO!

**VALERIE.** It's all right, Agnes…

*(**OWEN** prepares himself for his rape.)*

**AGNES.** Please…

**OWEN.** Please what?

**AGNES.** Please don't rape my sister…

**OWEN.** As much as I love to hear you beg, I AM going to rape your sister, Agnes. I'm going to rape her with my enormous cock. My enormous, completely straight cock that does not at all resemble any kind of salted nut.

*(**AGNES** struggles to remove her burka.)*

**OWEN.** Keep the fucking burka on.

*(**OWEN** begins to rape **VALERIE** as **AGNES** watches in horrified silence.)*

*(**AGNES** begins to cry.)*

**OWEN.** Look, your sister is crying! But you haven't cried once, Valerie. You are so dignified. You won't cry, will you?

**VALERIE.** No.

**OWEN.** I know you won't. You have too much class for that. You are dignified and heroic.

**VALERIE.** Thank you.

**OWEN.** You're welcome.

   (**OWEN** *continues his rape. He climaxes.*)

**OWEN.** I'm done raping you now, Valerie. You did very well.

**VALERIE.** Thank you.

**OWEN.** Now I'm going to stick a grenade in your vagina and I'm going to pull the pin. Okay?

**VALERIE.** Okay.

**OWEN.** Okay.

**AGNES.** You bastard!

   (**AGNES** *charges* **OWEN**. **OWEN** *smacks her down with the gun. Then he removes a grenade from his pocket.*)

**OWEN.** What I do here today, I do for the good of my country, my people, and all mankind.

   (*He sticks the grenade into* **VALERIE**'*s vagina. He closes his eyes.*)

   (*quietly*) Good night, Maestro.

   (*He pulls the pin. All three cringe.*)

   (*darkness*)

   (*After a long moment, a single light rises upon a chair, a bottle of water, and a microphone. Another long moment.*)

   (**OWEN** *enters, wearing a tweed jacket and glasses. He smiles and waves to the audience, mouthing the words "thank you" a few times. He is gracious and humble.*)

   (*Then he takes his seat. He smiles and waves again, takes a sip of his water, smiles and nods, laughs at something we don't hear. He leans into the mike.*)

**OWEN.** *(cont.)* Except when I'm sober.

*(He laughs, then waves the joke away.)*

'K, ah, I only have a few minutes, so…

*(He takes another sip of his water. He squints and points to someone in the audience.)*

Yes.

*(He leans forward, straining, as though he is listening to something someone is saying. He nods and then leans into the mike.)*

Ah. Great. I'm so glad you asked that question. Remember that huge story last year about the two girls who'd go to pro-life conventions and murder dudes, then write about it on their blog? I started writing about them, initially. But then I became fascinated by the war. And so the girls kind of morphed into this legion of pro-Iraq feminist insurgents. And it went from there.

*(He shields his eyes and points to someone else in the audience.)*

You, in the hat.

*(He cups his ear, listening, nodding, sipping his water. He leans into the mike.)*

Well I wouldn't say I have a "bleak" outlook on life, per se. But I do think humans are a pretty cruel bunch…As I see it, I'm not creating reprehensible characters, I'm merely giving voice to the unspoken.

*(He scans the audience and points to someone else.)*

You, yes.

*(He listens.)*

*(into the mike)* I certainly don't expect everyone to love it. This kind of work is polarizing. Some people don't want to see the truth. But my question to them is, why is "truth" so controversial? It's like a flock of geese… when you see them from afar in a field, they look great, they look beautiful, but if you go out in the field, it's covered with shit. And the geese are looking at that

shit saying, "Where did that come from?" Well we are knee deep in it right now, as a country. And THAT'S the truth. Like it or not.

*(He scans the audience and points to someone else.)*

**OWEN.** *(cont.)* Okay, you. Hi.

*(He listens.)*

*(into the mike)* Yes. My mother. She's sitting right there, actually. Hey, Mom. She's so cute.

*(He waves and laughs. He scans the audience and points to someone else. He listens.)*

*(into the mike)* Um, gosh. I never know how to answer that. Um, Jean–Luc Godard is an influence, definitely. Scorsese, uh…Mel Gibson, believe it or not…Woody Allen, David Lynch…I could go on.

*(He scans the audience and points to someone else.)*

Yes, in the back.

*(He listens.)*

*(into the mike)* That's kind of you to say. But honestly? I don't think of them as "female" characters. I think of them as people. I'm an observer of the human condition, irregardless of gender. I'm "gender blind," as they say.

*(**OWEN** acknowledges someone offstage as though they are telling him his time is almost up. He scans the audience and points to someone else.)*

One last question, yes.

*(He sips his water and listens.)*

*(This question has clearly blown his mind. He's at a loss. He leans into the mike. He opens his mouth to speak. He closes it. He opens it again. He closes it. He opens it again.)*

*(This goes on for a bit.)*

*(blackout)*

**End of Play**

# ABOUT THE PLAYWRIGHT

SHEILA CALLAGHAN'S plays have been produced and developed by Soho Rep, Playwrights Horizons, South Coast Repertory, Clubbed Thumb, Lark Play Development Center, Actors Theatre of Louisville, New Georges and the 2th Street Theatre, among others. Sheila's awards include the Princess Grace Works in Progress Award (2008), the Susan Smith Blackburn Prize (2007) and the prestigious Whiting Award (2007). Sheila has been the recipient of the Princess Grace fellowship for emerging artists (2000), a Jerome fellowship from the Playwrights Center in Minneapolis (2001), a MacDowell Colony residency (2003) and a Cherry Lane Mentorship fellowship (2005). She has received grants from NYFA, NYSCA and the MAP Foundation. Her plays have been produced in New Zealand, Norway, Germany and the Czech Republic. She has been commissioned by Playwrights Horizons, South Coast Repertory, Playwrights Foundation, Clubbed Thumb and EST/Sloan. Her full-length plays include *Scab, Crawl Fade to White, Crumble (Lay Me Down, Justin Timberlake), We Are Not These Hands, Dead City, Lascivious Something, Kate Crackernuts, That Pretty Pretty; or, The Rape Play* and *Fever/Dream*. Several of her plays are published by Playscripts and Samuel French, and her monologues can be found in various anthologies. She has taught playwriting at The University of Rochester, The College of New Jersey and Florida State University; she is currently on the faculty at Spalding University's MFA program in creative writing. Sheila is a resident artist at HERE Arts Center and a member of the OBIE-winning playwrights' organization, 13P. Sheila is also a resident of New Dramatists. Her play *Fever/Dream* will make its world premiere at Washington DC's Woolly Mammoth Theatre in June 2009 (Howard Stalwitz directs), and her play *Lascivious Something* will premiere at the Cherry Lane Theatre in August 2009 (Daniela Topol directs).

# From the Reviews of
# **THAT PRETTY PRETTY...**

"Mind-blowing images and soul-crushing language flowing wildly."
- *Back Stage*

"A submersion in the anarchy of ambivalence: variously a rant, a riff, a rumble - about our notions of naturalism, objectification, perversity, and beauty ... There's sass and sarcasm in Callaghan's high-energy punk writing."
- John Lahr, *The New Yorker*

"Raunchy, savvy... the twisted, caffeinated world of the show imagines the collective subconscious of a culture where girls never stiop going wild... [Callaghan] push(es) her audience's buttons with an aggressive treatment of some of the darker corners of the human psyche."
- *The New York Times*

**Also by
Sheila Callaghan...**

**Ayravana Flies, or A Pretty Dish**

**Crawl, Fade to White**

**Dead City**

**We Are Not These Hands**

**Scab**

Please visit our website **samuelfrench.com** for complete descriptions and licensing information